Caillou

Lights Out!

Adaptation from the animated series: Anne Paradis
Illustrations taken from the animated series and adapted by Eric Sevigny

chouette

One evening, Caillou was playing in the living room. Daddy was watching TV, and Gilbert was looking out the window. "Meow!"
"Do you want to go outside, Gilbert?" Caillou asked.
"Why don't you let him out?" Daddy said.
Caillou got up and saw huge swirls of snow outside.

"Daddy, look!"
Caillou was amazed by the wind and heavy snow.
He knew that tomorrow would be a great day to build
a snowman.
"The weatherman said there would be a storm tonight.
I'd better turn up the heat. Why don't we go and see if
Mommy needs help setting the table?" Daddy asked.

Gilbert was waiting to go out. When Caillou opened the door, the wind blasted in.

"What an awful storm!" Mommy said.

"And it looks like it's getting worse," Daddy answered.

"Well, there's no use worrying about something we can't control!" Mommy added. "Why don't you go wash up for supper, Caillou?"

Caillou went to wash his hands. He wondered why
Mommy and Daddy were so worried about the storm.
The bathroom lights began to flicker.
"Hey!" Caillou was surprised.
Then the lights went out. Caillou tried to turn them back
on, but they didn't work.
Caillou felt very alone in the dark. "Daddy!"

Caillou felt better when he heard Daddy's voice. "I'm coming, Caillou. Stay where you are! The storm must have caused a power failure."

"What's that?" Caillou asked.

Daddy explained, "A power failure is when there's no electricity, so the lights don't work."

"But we need lights," Caillou said.

"Let's go get the flashlights in the basement," Daddy answered.

First Caillou and Daddy went into the kitchen to get some candles. "It's pitch black down there. These will help us see."

Caillou sat on the stairs while Daddy looked. "I guess it isn't the best place to keep the flashlights, is it?" Daddy laughed.

"Be careful, Daddy," Caillou said. He felt a bit scared alone on the stairs.

Suddenly, it was completely dark.

"Oh, no! My candle blew out. I'm sure the flashlights were right here."

Caillou was frightened in the dark stairwell all by himself.

"Found them!" Daddy exclaimed.

An odd shape appeared in front of Caillou. "Oh!"

It was Daddy making a face with the flashlight.

Caillou was happy that there were lights again. He liked to play with the flashlights.

Gilbert chased the light on the floor.

"I'll try to fix us a meal," Mommy said.

"I'll get some wood and build a fire. We can heat something in the fireplace, just like when we're camping!"

The family was gathered by the fireplace.

"I like camping in the living room," Caillou said.

"Yes, it's fun, but I hope the electricity comes back on soon. The house is getting a little chilly."

"When will the lights come back on?" Caillou asked.

"I'm not sure, Caillou. It could take some time," Daddy answered.

After supper, Daddy asked, "What's your favorite dessert when we go camping?"
"Marshmallows!" Caillou replied.
Yum! They were even better toasted in the fireplace!

Caillou yawned. "I think it's bedtime," Mommy said. Caillou didn't want to sleep alone in his dark room. Daddy said, "Why don't we all sleep down here tonight!"

Caillou was asleep by the fire in the living room.
Suddenly the sound of the TV woke him up. "The power's back on," Daddy said.
Caillou got up to turn off the TV. "Can we still sleep here tonight, Daddy?"
"Sure! Goodnight, Caillou."
Caillou got right back into his sleeping bag. The living room was the best campground ever!

Text: adaptation by Anne Paradis of the animated series CAILLOU,
produced by DHX Media Inc.
All rights reserved.
Original script written by Natalie Dumoulin.
Original episode #72 Lights Out
Illustrations: Eric Sévigny, based on the animated series CAILLOU

The PBS KIDS logo is a registered mark of PBS and is used with permission.

We acknowledge the financial support of the Government of Canada through
the Canada Book Fund for our publishing activities.

Canadian   Patrimoine
Heritage   canadien

We acknowledge the support of the Ministry of Culture and Communications
of Quebec and SODEC for the publication and promotion of this book.

SODEC
  Québec

Bibliothèque et Archives nationales du Québec and Library and Archives
Canada cataloguing in publication

Paradis, Anne, 1972-
Caillou: Lights Out!
(Playtime)
For children aged 3 and up.

ISBN 978-2-89718-203-8

I. Sévigny, Éric. II. Title. III. Title: Lights Out! IV. Series: Playtime (Montréal,
Québec).

PS8631.A713C332 2015   jC813'.6   C2015-940244-1
PS9631.A713C332 2015

Printed in China
10 9 8 7 6 5 4 3 2 1 CHO1938 MAY2015